WINNER OF THE RUTH SCHWARTZ MEMORIAL AWARD
FOR BEST CHILDREN'S BOOK OF 1976

In the story Chris saves his pennies to buy a violin. When he tries to play it, the violin makes such nasty squeaks that he throws it away. An old man finds the violin in a wastebasket and when he plays, the violin makes the loveliest sounds ever heard. Chris wants his violin back.

"I really didn't throw it away," he tells his best friend Danny. "I just put it there for a while."

A child's love of music is revealed in this poignant tale of a boy's longing and an old man's generosity.

"Richly produced . . . rare and moving . . . the story is simplicity itself"
STEPHEN LEWIS—*The Globe & Mail*

"Stunning photographs . . . the characters are beautiful" —*Saturday Night*

"A heartwarming story . . . destined to become one of those treasured books of childhood" MICHAEL O. NOWLAN—*Fredericton Daily Gleaner*

"Here is a treasure" —*Lethbridge Herald*

"A captivating book on the love of music, the search for dreams . . . a delight to readers of all ages" —*Kingston Whig-Standard*

"Beautifully done" —*Canadian Composer*

ROBERT THOMAS ALLEN is one of Canada's best-known writers – author of many books and twice winner of the Leacock Award for humor. He also wrote the narrative for the film *The Violin* on which this book is based.

MAURICE SOLWAY, the internationally acclaimed concert violinist, plays the role of the violinist in this story. His theme music (included in this book) from the film *The Violin* earned him the coveted Canadian Film and Television Award. The photographs by GEORGE PASTIC were taken during the making of the film.

THE VIOLIN

THE VIOLIN

From the story by George Pastic and Andrew Welsh

text by
Robert Thomas Allen

photography by
George Pastic

Featuring Maurice Solway as the old man

McGraw-Hill Ryerson Limited

Toronto   Montreal   New York
London   Sydney   Johannesburg
Mexico   Panama   Düsseldorf   Kuala Lumpur
São Paulo   New Delhi   Auckland

THE VIOLIN

Copyright © McGraw-Hill Ryerson Limited, 1976.

Story by Andrew Welsh and George Pastic, from the film *The Violin* produced by Sincinkin Limited.

First paperback edition 1977
ISBN 0-07-082620-X
2 3 4 5 6 7 8 9 0 BP 5 4 3 2 1 0 9 8
Printed and bound in Canada

his story happened not very long ago on an island. It wasn't an island far out in the sea. It was an island in the harbour of a big city. Yet it was a real island, quiet and peaceful. In the winter cottontail rabbits hopped across the frozen lagoons.

Chris and Danny lived on the island all winter. They were great friends and played together in the snow and had a secret hiding place.

It was the hollow of a big willow tree.

Chris, the older boy, who was often quiet and thoughtful, had been saving his money for a long time. He knew that now there should be enough to buy the wonderful thing that he had been longing to have.

On this special morning Chris reached into the tree and felt around.

"Is it there?" Danny asked.

Chris took a jar full of coins from the tree. He held it up and jingled it and dropped a few more coins into the jar. There was enough! Anyway the boys thought there was enough.

The two boys began to shout. They danced in the snow, and ran from the woods — through an old garden of an empty cottage, down the path to the docks, over the gangplank onto the ferryboat that was smoking and puffing ready to take islanders across the bay to the city.

The boom of the ferryboat's horn sounded as if it were telling the very clouds that something important was going to happen this day.

By this time, as he often did, Danny looked as if he were coming apart. His mother sometimes pinned his mitts to his coat, looking him in the eye saying, "Now don't lose these, Danny," but he usually lost them anyway.

Chris stood at the rail as the boat moved across the water. He looked serious now that his dream was soon to come true. Danny asked, "How do you know you can play it when you get it, Chris?"

"I know I can," Chris said.

The people on the busy streets hurried along looking straight ahead as if there were nothing special in the store windows. But the window the boys finally reached and gazed into was a magic world, like a stage. The winter sun shone on a patch of faded blue cloth. An orange cat was asleep in the corner and there in the middle was the magic object that Chris had wanted for such a long time, graceful and shiny as a new chestnut —

a violin.

It looked so beautiful that Chris stood for a moment outside the door to the store, hardly able to believe that soon it would be his own.

When he opened the door, a man looked up from behind the counter. Chris handed him the jar of coins to pay for the violin — the one in the window. But life is full of disappointments, and grown-ups sometimes make things worse with awful jokes.

"Oho! So you want to buy an expensive violin with a jar full of pennies and dimes?" The man looked at the jar of coins as if he didn't think very much of it. "By the time you save enough nickels for *that* violin you'll have a long grey beard."

Chris just stared. But Danny was anxious to help. He told the man that he could have other things besides the money and began taking his prized possessions from his pockets — pictures of birds, a shiny alley, a hawk's foot. The man looked at them as if nothing in life would ever interest him again.

"Chicken's feet I don't need," he said.

"It's a hawk's foot."

"I don't need hawks' feet either. With hawks' feet I can't pay the rent."

Sometimes, though, people aren't as mean as they first seem. When the boys started to leave, the man called to them, "Just a minute now. There was one — let me think." He shifted some things around on a bottom shelf and held up another violin so Chris could see it. "Here. This one has everything the other one has — strings, a bow, a place to put your chin. It's a better one for a boy. I can let you have it for the money in the jar."

On the way home on the ferry, holding the violin, Chris felt somehow that the world had changed. He couldn't believe that the violin the man had sold him was as good as the one he had seen at first. Nothing would cheer him up, not even looking at Danny. Chris had dreamt of owning and playing a violin ever since one day he went with his mother to a concert. He never forgot how he felt when a boy no older than he was came out and played a violin. Beautiful sounds seemed to fall from the air inside the concert hall.

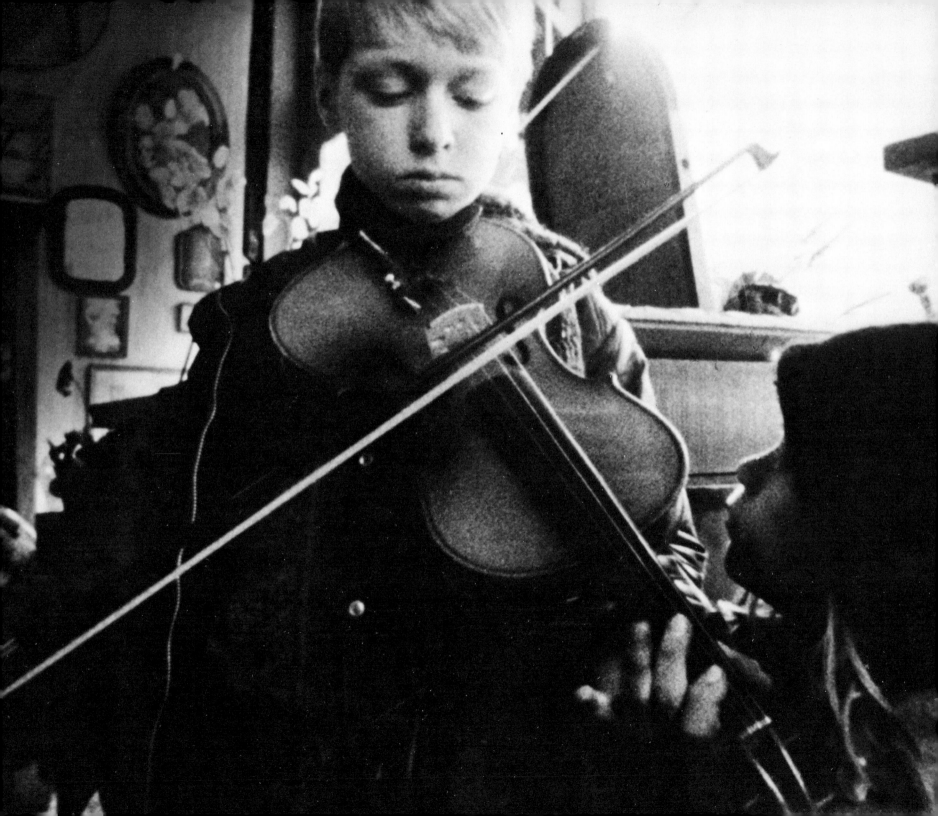

When they were back home, Chris took the violin from the case and put it under his chin. He could almost hear the hush of a huge audience waiting for him to play. He drew the bow across the strings. But the sound that came from the violin was nothing like the music in Chris's head. It was like a squeaking door, or perhaps a growling pup.

Danny went outside and put his hands over his ears. Soon afterwards, Chris came out of the cottage and sat down beside Danny on the step.

"This violin is no good," he said. He put the violin in its case and walked away from the cottage. Danny followed him.

When he came to a wire wastebasket, he dropped the violin in among the old newspapers. He felt better, but not much. It was snowing and he began to make a snowball to throw at Danny but he noticed that Danny was watching something in the distance.

A man was coming along the path — a strange-looking man, wearing a black coat and a kind of high black hat Chris had never seen before. As he moved through the snow his coat flapped and he looked like a big crow that had decided to walk instead of fly. Chris and Danny watched him sit down on the park bench; then the man looked into the basket and lifted out the violin.

He opened the case and took out the violin. The way he tightened the bow and tuned the strings and put the violin under his chin, like something he was trying to warm up, you could tell he was used to violins.

"But the man has not heard *that* violin!" Chris whispered to Danny, "I wonder what he'll do when he hears the awful sound it makes?"

But when the man began to play, with the snow falling around him, Chris knew that he had never heard such beautiful music. The boys came right up behind the bench where the man was playing, but he was so lost in his music that he didn't notice them. Chris knew now that it wasn't the fault of the violin when it made terrible sounds; it just needed someone who knew how to play it. He wanted his violin back.

"I didn't really throw it away," Chris whispered to Danny, "I just put it there for a while." Which shows you how easy it is to believe anything you want to believe, even when it isn't true.

The man put the violin back in its case and started to walk away with it. Chris and Danny followed him. What would the man do, Chris wondered, when he asked for the violin back? Would the man turn around and yell or maybe even take a swing at them with the violin case?

Danny never seemed to worry about things like that and when they caught up with the man, Danny just tugged his sleeve and said, "That's our violin."

Chris began to tell the man why the violin was in the wastebasket. The man peered at him over his glasses and smiled, and seemed so glad of their company, that Chris knew he would give him not only the violin but almost anything. The man told them where his cottage was.

"I'll take the violin home with me," he said. "I'll polish it and tune it. If you tell your mothers where you're going, you can come over and get it."

The old man's cottage was the most wonderful place. It had the same look that Chris liked about Danny — nice and friendly but falling apart. Magazines and books had fallen off shelves. There were piles of sheet music where there should have been cups and plates and there were cups and plates on top of sheet music. There was a pet rabbit on the table and a pigeon in a cage. Things fell from strange places if you jiggled anything. "Never mind picking them up," the man would say. A pink umbrella fell off a bookcase.

"Don't bother picking it up," the man said. "I found that. I use it as a sunshade when I go out in my rowboat."

You could have lost Danny among the things that the man hadn't put away in their proper place. Chris asked the man if he'd play the violin for him again. This time the man played a different tune — light and fast and kind of funny.

He played to the pigeon. He played to the rabbit. He played to Chris and Danny. It looked so easy that Chris wanted to try again, but he made such a squawking sound that Danny put his hands over his ears and went outside.

Chris knew now that he *did* want to learn to play the violin after all. The man showed him how the violin was made, and told him something of its special place among instruments. A violinist can make almost as many sounds with a violin as a singer can with the human voice, playing notes that are very low and very high, making music sad or soft, light, gentle, bright, or strong.

Violins, the man said, were first made over four hundred years ago in the small town of Cremona in northern Italy. One maker was Antonius Stradivarius, who made the finest violins of his time.

The man showed Chris how to hold the violin and how to draw the bow across the strings. When he did it, he made a wonderful, sweet sound. When Chris tried, he made a sound like wood splitting, but before he left the man told him to come back and he would teach him how to play.

uring the following months when he gave Chris lessons, he sometimes looked off into space, as if his thoughts were thousands of miles away. He'd say "I remember one time…" and tell of something that happened long ago. Gradually Chris formed a picture in his mind of a mountain village and peaks that turned gold in the sun, and of big cities and after-theatre parties, and a bright far-off world where people loved music and talked music and lived for music. Then something had happened that sent the man wandering into strange lands with his violin.

The snow began to thaw, and by the time the lake had turned pale blue and the willows looked like green fountains, the man seemed pleased with his pupil. On warm days he and Chris played duets sitting on the rocks by the shore of the lake.

The man talked more and more often now of the mountains he had known as a boy and he was sometimes far away in his thoughts. Once when Chris told him he'd never want to be without his violin — the one he once threw away — the man looked at him a long time and then said, "We sometimes become too attached to things." He looked down at his own violin. "This is like an old friend to me, but if I had to part with it, I wouldn't stop loving music."

Chris thought it a strange thing to say, but then forgot about it because he and Danny and the man were having so much fun together. They took rides on the ferryboat and went on picnics. Sometimes the man lay in the grass just looking up at the blue sky, listening to Chris play his violin.

They went to the zoo where Danny ran around as if he knew each of the animals personally. Chris saw the animals as if they were not in the zoo at all: the camels in long dusty caravans moving across the desert, the deer in a northern forest, the fox crossing a dewy meadow at dawn when the woods seem to float on a morning mist.

Chris knew his violin like a friendly face. He knew there was a chip out of one of the pegs which tighten the strings and a little dark swirl in the grain of the wood seemed to watch him like a friendly eye as he played.

Yet in a strange way, when he played down by the wooden bridge in the soft sunlight of late summer, he felt a bit sad. The lonely rustle of the cottonwood trees, or the way a leaf fell beside him, like a tear, seemed to tell him that a time comes when friends must part.

One day Chris and Danny were on the bridge. Chris had his violin. Danny was fishing — his kind of fishing — catching minnows in a net tied to the end of a line, so that he could put them in a jar of water and look at them. Just as Chris started to play his favorite piece, Danny called out, "It's stuck!" He was tugging on his fishing line.

"Wait a minute," Chris said, "I'll help you." He put his violin down and went to help. But Danny didn't want help even from Chris. "Leave it alone!"

Chris caught hold of the pole. Danny butted him with his head.

"Stop it. Stop it!" Chris said. Grabbing Danny, he fell backward, laughing.

There was an awful cracking sound.

Chris took the violin from the case. It was a terrible sight: crushed and splintered, its strings limp like the wrappings of an open parcel. For Chris it was as if a cloud had passed over the sun. Danny was talking anxiously beside him, saying, "I'll fix it, Chris, I'll nail it together. I'll glue it together. I'll buy you a new one."

"I'll never play a violin again," Chris said, and wouldn't say any more.

Chris leaned against the railing of the bridge. His stomach felt sore with sadness. He didn't even look up when he heard Danny racing down the steps. He didn't know, or care, that Danny was racing off to find the man and tell him about the accident. Danny was sure the man would know what to do to help.

When he got to the man's cottage Danny found a note on the door. He could read a few words. He read "Dear Boys" and he knew the man had written it for them and that he wasn't there. Where had he gone?

Danny knew the man often went for a walk along the lakeshore. He pulled the note off the door and ran towards the lake as fast as he could.

When Danny found the man he said all in one breath, "I broke the violin. I mean Chris broke it, but I shoved him. He's sitting on the bridge. He said he'd never play again."

At first the man looked at him sadly as if he didn't hear. He spoke as if to himself "Chris mustn't say that." Then he said, "Wait here for a minute, Danny. I'd like to talk to Chris alone," and began to walk anxiously toward the bridge.

Danny felt sure the man would know what to do. But sometimes grown-ups aren't sure what to do. Walking towards the bridge, the man knew he had to make a difficult decision. He had owned his violin for a long, long time. But it wasn't because it was a very special violin that the decision was so hard to make. It was because he wasn't sure that his decision would help Chris. A gift for music is only a beginning. It takes years of hard work to become a musician. But he could think of nothing else to do; the man went up the steps.

Chris looked up and saw the man standing in front of him in his strange coat and hat, his face kind of sagging with worry. "Danny told me what happened," the man said. He held his own violin out to Chris. "This is yours now. I can get another — some day. But only you know whether you will go on and practice and work hard to become a fine musician."

Chris just shook his head. His throat felt tight. He couldn't speak. He never wanted to play a violin again — any violin. The feeling of knowing that he could play had come to an end.

The man went down the steps and stood for a long time on the path, looking very thoughtful. Then he put his violin on the bottom step, picked up the pigeon cage and his other things and walked slowly away.

Chris just sat there. The man had been gone a few minutes when Danny raced up the bridge calling, "Chris! Chris!" He handed the letter to Chris. "I found this nailed to his door. He's gone. The pigeon is gone. The rabbit is gone. We may never see him again."

Chris ran down off the bridge. Danny started after him, then turned and picked up the violin the man had left for Chris. He caught up with Chris as he ran through the woods.

"Where will he be?" Danny asked.

"I don't know."

They reached the old willow tree where they once hid their jar of coins, long ago last winter.

Chris climbed up into the branches and looked around.

"I see him! Over there. In his boat. He's rowing out from shore."

They raced down a path through the woods and faded
gardens and along a boardwalk. They reached the rocks on
the shore where Chris and the man had played their duets.
The man was out on the lake in his boat, rowing with the
pink umbrella shading the pigeon and rabbit. He was too
far out to hear the boys' shouts, or perhaps too far away in
his thoughts.

Then Chris felt Danny nudge him with the violin. Chris knew what Danny meant. Perhaps music would be the only thing the man could hear. He thought of his own old violin lying broken on the bridge. He had never played another violin and was afraid he would make the same squawking sounds on this violin that he made when he first tried to play his own. Yet the violin felt just right under his chin. He began to play a tune the man had taught him.

As Chris played, he felt as though the man were beside him once again. The music soared out over the blue water, as light and graceful as a seagull gliding on a summer breeze.

"He hears you!" shouted Danny.

Danny was crying, "We won't ever see him again."
Chris pretended he didn't hear Danny.

Later he'd tell him that nobody ever says goodbye who leaves the world beautiful music.

REMINISCENCE

Music by Maurice Solway

Reminiscence 2